we ♥ you just the way you are!

Dedicated to all of you that have never given up!

Especially to my incredible family. Thank you for never giving up and supporting me through this process. I love you all so very much.

x

Our aim with the Silly Eric books is to support street children around the globe. We do this by giving a percentage of each book sale to a children's charity. Thank you for joining in and supporting the children of the future.

© 2018 Gracie Wright

Miss Wright Publishing LTD

info@misswrightpublishing.com

For more information on our children's camp, workshops and Silly Eric products go to www.sillyeric.co.uk

ISBN-10: 0993108067
ISBN-13: 978-0993108068

Written and concept design by Gracie Wright
Illustrated by Brandon Mattless
Edited by Graham Marks

Dedicated to

...Minnie McDowall...

Sometimes, when Eric found himself muddled up with too many thoughts, life could be a little bit challenging.

But he never gave up!

Today was test day at Eric's school and he was practising at home with Birdy and Mr Orange.

"2 + 2 is?" said Birdy. "4!" said Eric.
"3 + 3 is?" asked Mr Orange.
"Sticks!" said Eric.

2 + 2 =
3 + 3 =

Silly Eric, it's six not sticks.
Try again!

Eric packed his bag with everything he needed and was ready to go. But wait a second, Eric suddenly remembered he had never ridden his bike on his own before.

Maybe he should go back and get his scooter?

Come on Silly Eric, give it a try!

Off he went with his head held high,
but then, Oh no! He tumbled off!

"Never mind", he said, getting up again,
"Silly Eric never gives up!"

He wibbled a bit, and wobbled some more,
the longer Eric stayed on the
easier it got.

"Not giving up was easier than I thought," he said.

The English test was first and the teacher asked them all to spell the word 'elephant'.

Eric carefully wrote down ELAFUNT,
but realised it didn't look quite right.

Remember all the practice you did, try again.
Silly Eric never gives up!

Out of the blue a picture popped into Eric's head and he remembered what he should have written!

whoo-hoo!

elafunt

He rubbed out ELAFUNT and wrote down ELEPHANT instead.

Well done Eric!

Next it was his Maths test.
"If you have two apples," said the teacher, "and your friend has five apples, how many apples are there?"

Pictures of apples kept popping up into his thoughts and he couldn't think of the answer.

Oh no! He was now covered in apples!

Eric concentrated as hard as he could.
Squeezing his eyes tightly shut he counted on
his fingers the apples he saw.

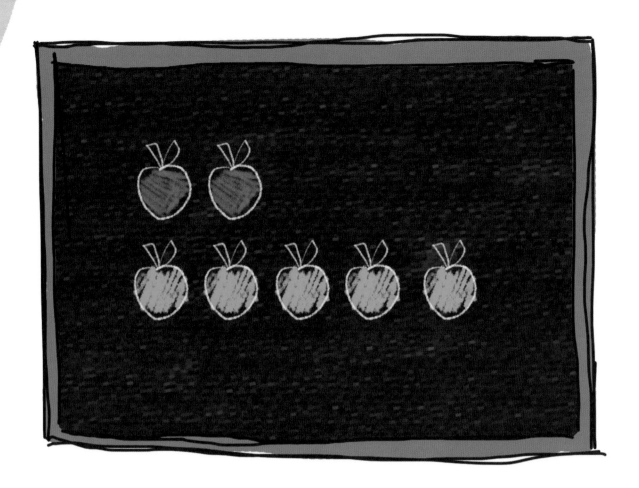

1... 2... 3... 4... 5... 6... and 7!

"Nothing's too difficult when you never give up!" shouted Eric.

Then they all went outside for a race.
"Ready... steady... GO!" announced his teacher.

Eric ran as fast as he could but he fell flat on
his face! Oh no! His laces were tied together!

"Keep going Eric!"
the teacher shouted,
"Silly Eric never gives up!"

After lunch it was reading time and
Silly Eric was afraid he might say
the words the wrong way round.

Silly Eric, just turn the book the right way round!

You're a good reader!

The last test was Art, which Eric loved but he didn't know how to finish the family picture.

And then he had a great idea!

"That's perfect Eric," said his teacher,

"Your Dad's eyebrows are very bushy!"

Eric rode home, not wibbling or
wobbling once and bounced into the house,
handing his test results to his mum!

"Well done Eric!"
she cheered,
"Your teacher gave you a gold star for never giving up!"

The End.

Colour me in!

Share your picture on social media using
#SillyEricComp
for your chance to win a Silly Eric product!

Join the fun...

Share your Silly Eric
pictures and videos at:

📷 @SillyEricBook

🐦 @SillyEricTweets

f facebook.com/SillyEricBook

▶️ Silly Eric

www.sillyeric.co.uk

Also available in the Silly Eric range

Kids T-shirts Age 2-13 from £15
or have it custom-made with your name!
#NameNeverGivesUp

Buy yours now at

www.sillyeric.co.uk

Printed in Great Britain
by Amazon